Rainbow Edition

Reading Mastery II
Behavioral Objectives

Siegfried Engelmann • Elaine C. Bruner

SRA

SRA/McGraw-Hill
8787 Orion Place
Columbus, OH 43240-4027
Printed in the United States of America.
ISBN 0-02-686352-9

9 0 IPC 02 01

INTRODUCTION

The *Reading Mastery* program is based on the underlying concept that all children can learn if carefully taught. The program provides the kind of careful instruction that is needed to teach basic reading skills.

The sequence of skills in *Reading Mastery II* is controlled so that the student is able to perform confidently the skills at each step before going on to more complicated tasks. The program builds on the skills developed in *Reading Mastery I* and also teaches new concepts in the following areas: sound-letter relationships, decoding, letter names, alphabetical order, decoding, reading vocabulary, following directions, oral reading, and comprehension.

In addition, students have an opportunity to improve and expand independent work skills through take-home activities. In take-homes for picture and reading comprehension, written exercises relate to stories or factual passages that the students read. Other take-home activities include sound writing, sentence copying, following written instructions, and deductive thinking.

In spelling, an optional part of the program, the students learn to spell first by sounds and later by letter names. They also learn to write sounds, sound combinations, words, and sentences.

Scope and Sequence Chart
The Scope and Sequence chart on page 2 provides a quick overview of *Reading Mastery II*. The chart lists the various tracks (skills) that are taught and the range of lessons for each track.

Behavioral Objectives
This booklet gives a comprehensive picture of *Reading Mastery II*. It focuses on the general curriculum goals of the program and on special behavioral goals to be achieved by individual students.

The Behavioral Objectives, which begin on page 3, cover the major skill areas, or tracks, shown on the Scope and Sequence chart. Above each chart is the name of the track and the range of lessons in which it appears. The chart itself is divided into four sections:

• The **Purpose of the track** is the general curriculum objective.

• The **Behavioral objective** is the kind of performance that can be expected from the student who has mastered the skill.

• The section headed **The student is asked to** describes the specific kinds of tasks the student performs in order to master the skill.

• The section headed **First appears in** shows where the skill is first introduced in the program.

SCOPE AND SEQUENCE CHART

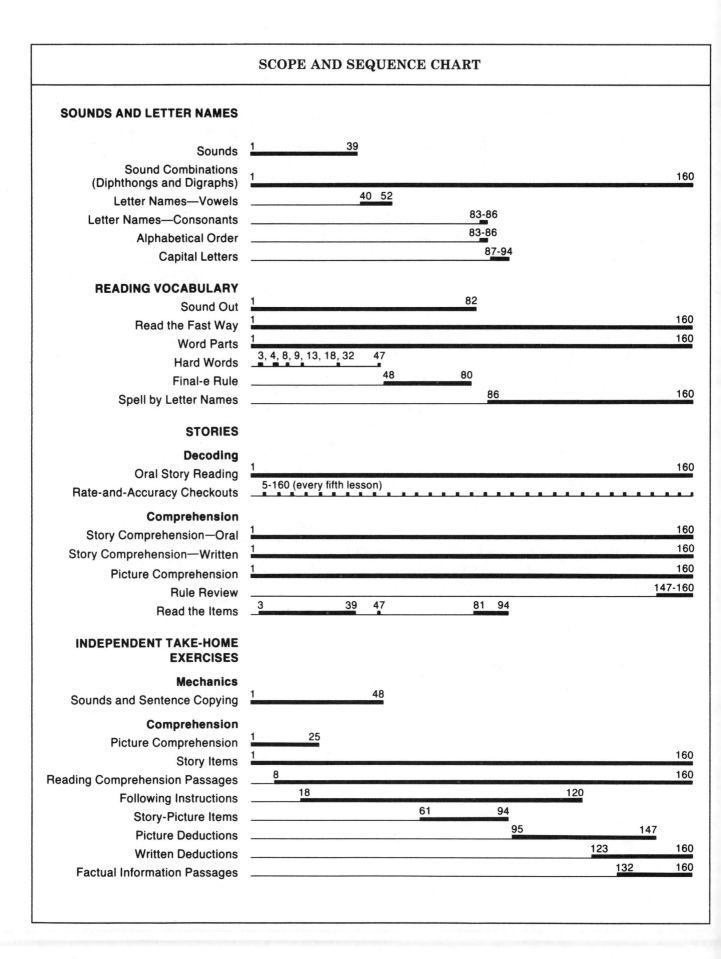

SOUNDS AND LETTER NAMES

Sounds — 1 — 39

Sound Combinations (Diphthongs and Digraphs) — 1 — 160

Letter Names—Vowels — 40 52

Letter Names—Consonants — 83-86

Alphabetical Order — 83-86

Capital Letters — 87-94

READING VOCABULARY

Sound Out — 1 — 82

Read the Fast Way — 1 — 160

Word Parts — 1 — 160

Hard Words — 3, 4, 8, 9, 13, 18, 32 47

Final-e Rule — 48 — 80

Spell by Letter Names — 86 — 160

STORIES

Decoding

Oral Story Reading — 1 — 160

Rate-and-Accuracy Checkouts — 5-160 (every fifth lesson)

Comprehension

Story Comprehension—Oral — 1 — 160

Story Comprehension—Written — 1 — 160

Picture Comprehension — 1 — 160

Rule Review — 147-160

Read the Items — 3 — 39 47 — 81 94

INDEPENDENT TAKE-HOME EXERCISES

Mechanics

Sounds and Sentence Copying — 1 — 48

Comprehension

Picture Comprehension — 1 — 25

Story Items — 1 — 160

Reading Comprehension Passages — 8 — 160

Following Instructions — 18 — 120

Story-Picture Items — 61 — 94

Picture Deductions — 95 — 147

Written Deductions — 123 — 160

Factual Information Passages — 132 — 160

SOUNDS: SOUND RECOGNITION   **Range of Lessons: 1-39**

Purpose of the track	Behavioral objectives	The student is asked to	First appears in
To review the sounds taught in *Reading Mastery I*	When given a printed symbol, the student is able to recognize and produce the sound represented by the symbol.	Say the sounds represented by the following symbols:	

Symbol	Sound	As in	
a	aaa	and	Lesson 1
u	uuu	under	Lesson 1
th	thththth	this (not thing)	Lesson 1
e	eee	end	Lesson 1
wh	whwhwh	why	Lesson 1
d	d	dad	Lesson 1
o	ooo	ox	Lesson 1
h	hhh	hat	Lesson 1
i	iii	if	Lesson 1
sh	shshsh	she	Lesson 2
ī	$\bar{\text{iii}}$	ice	Lesson 2
ō	$\overline{\text{ooo}}$	over	Lesson 3
m	mmm	mat	Lesson 3
ch	ch	chat	Lesson 3
ē	$\overline{\text{eee}}$	eat	Lesson 4
g	g	go	Lesson 4
l	lll	late	Lesson 4
s	sss	sat	Lesson 4

(continued)

3

Purpose of the track	Behavioral objectives	The student is asked to	First appears in
		Say the sounds represented by the following symbols:	

Symbol	Sound	As in	First appears in
t	t	tap	Lesson 4
b	b	bag	Lesson 5
f	fff	fat	Lesson 5
r	rrr	rat	Lesson 5
x	x	ox	Lesson 6
$\bar{a}$	$\bar{a}\bar{a}\bar{a}$	ate	Lesson 7
$\bar{u}$	$\bar{u}\bar{u}\bar{u}$	use	Lesson 7
c	ccc	cat	Lesson 7
w	www	we	Lesson 8
n	nnn	nap	Lesson 9
$\bar{y}$	$\bar{y}\bar{y}\bar{y}$	yes	Lesson 11
p	ppp	pat	Lesson 11
z	zzz	zoo	Lesson 12
v	vvv	very	Lesson 12
k	k	kick	Lesson 14
y	yyy	my	Lesson 15
qu	qu	quick	Lesson 19
$\overline{ing}$	ing	sing	Lesson 19
er	er	brother	Lesson 19
j	j	jump	Lesson 20

Purpose of the track	Behavioral objectives	The student is asked to	First appears in
To teach the student letter sound combinations that make one sound		Identify the following sound combinations: Sound Combinations As in	
	Sound Combinations: When given a sound combination, the student is able to say the sound represented by the letters and to read words that contain the sound combination.	ar are	Lesson 1
		al all	Lesson 34
		ou out	Lesson 45
		ea eat	Lesson 81
		ee need	Lesson 83
	Disjoined letters: When given two or three letters that had previously been joined, the student is able to say the sound represented by the letters and to read words that contain the letters.	th this	Lesson 67
		sh she	Lesson 72
		ing sing	Lesson 76
		oo moon	Lesson 80
		wh why	Lesson 81
		ch chat	Lesson 81
		qu quick	Lesson 81
		er brother	Lesson 81

LETTER NAMES   **Range of Lessons: 40-86**

Purpose of the track	Behavioral objectives	The student is asked to	First appears in
To teach the student to identify the names of lowercase letters	*Vowels:* When given lowercase vowels, the student is able to identify each letter by name.	Say the names of the vowels *a*, *e*, *i*, *o*, and *u*	Lesson 40
	Consonants: When given lowercase consonants, the student is able to identify each letter by name.	Say the names of the consonants	Lesson 83

ALPHABETICAL ORDER   **Range of Lessons: 83-86**

Purpose of the track	Behavioral objectives	The student is asked to	First appears in
To teach the student to say the names of the letters of the alphabet in order	When given all of the alphabet, the student is able to say the names of the letters in order.	Say the names of the letters in order	Lesson 83

CAPITAL LETTERS   **Range of Lessons: 87-94**

Purpose of the track	Behavioral objectives	The student is asked to	First appears in
To teach the student to identify the names of capital letters	When given capital letters, the student is able to identify each letter by name.	Identify "easy" capitals (letters that are similar to their lowercase counterparts)	Lesson 87
		Identify "hard" capitals (letters that are very different from their lowercase counterparts)	Lesson 89

READING VOCABULARY: SOUND OUT   **Range of Lessons: 1-82**

Purpose of the track	Behavioral objectives	The student is asked to	First appears in
To teach the student to decode words	When given a word, the student is able to sound out the word and then say it at a normal rate.	Sound out a word and tell what word	Lesson 1

Purpose of the track	Behavioral objectives	The student is asked to	First appears in
To teach the student to read words without decoding them first	When given a word, the student is able to say the word at a normal rate without sounding it out first.	Identify a word	Lesson 1

Purpose of the track	Behavioral objectives	The student is asked to	First appears in
To teach the student to analyze parts of a word	*Last-part, first-part*: When given a word beginning with a consonant blend, the student is able to blend the beginning sound with the rest of the word and then to say it the fast way.	Read a word with the initial consonant covered, blend the initial consonant with the rest of the word, and say the whole word	Lesson 10
	Two-part words: When given a two-part word, the student is able to read the first part while the last part is covered and then to read the entire word.	Tell what the first part of a word says and then tell what the whole word says	Lesson 36
	Underlined parts: When given a word (a compound word, a word with a sound combination, a word with an ending, or a word that follows the long- vowel rule with endings), the student is able to read part of the word and then read the whole word.	Read the underlined part of a word and then read the whole word	Lesson 81

READING VOCABULARY: HARD WORDS   **Range of Lessons: 3-47**

Purpose of the track	Behavioral objectives	The student is asked to	First appears in
To give the student extra practice with words that often cause difficulty	When a list of hard words is presented, the student is able to read the words the fast way.	Read a list of words from the presentation book as a group and then read the same words from the storybook individually	Lesson 3

READING VOCABULARY: LISTEN, SOUND-OUT   **Range of Lessons: 10-80**

Purpose of the track	Behavioral objectives	The student is asked to	First appears in
To introduce irregular words that are sounded out one way and pronounced another way	When an irregular word is presented, the student is able both to sound out the word as it is spelled and to pronounce the word as it is said.	Repeat an irregular word read by the teacher, sound out the word, and then say the word	Lesson 10

Purpose of the track	Behavioral objectives	The student is asked to	First appears in
To teach the student to read long-vowel words ending in final *e*	*Read long-vowel words with final e*: When the final *e* rule has been presented, the student is able to recognize and read a long-vowel word with a final *e*.	Say the long-vowel sound of a word with a final *e* and read the word the fast way	Lesson 48
		Recognize a word with a final *e*, say the long-vowel sound, and read the word the fast way	Lesson 51
		After being prompted on the rule, read a long-vowel word with a final *e* the fast way and then sound out the word and say the word	Lesson 57
		After being prompted on the rule, read a long-vowel word with a final *e* the fast way	Lesson 57
		Read a long-vowel word with a final *e* the fast way	Lesson 60
	Discriminate between long- and short-vowel words: When given a vowel pair (a long-vowel word and a short-vowel word, such as **ate** and **at**) the student is able to discriminate between the long-vowel and short-vowel sounds and read the pair of words.	Reread a pair of long- and short- vowel words the fast way	Lesson 48
		Recognize whether each word in a vowel pair has a final *e*, say the sound of each vowel, and read each word the fast way	Lesson 51
		Read separate columns of long-vowel and short-vowel words, and then reread a mix of long- and short-vowel words	Lesson 54
		Recognize the word in a vowel pair that has a long vowel sound, and then read both words the fast way	Lesson 57
		Read a mix of long- and short-vowel words after being prompted on the final *e* rule	Lesson 63

READING VOCABULARY: SPELL BY LETTER NAMES   Range of Lessons: 86-160

Purpose of the track	Behavioral objectives	The student is asked to	First appears in
To teach the student to focus on every letter in a word	When a column of words is presented, the student is able to spell each word in the column by letter names and then read each word in the column.	Spell each word in a column of words and then read the column of words. (The teacher models the first three words)	Lesson 86
	When a word is presented, the student is able to spell the word by letter names and then read the word.	Spell a word and then read it the fast way	Lesson 88
	When a word is read by the teacher, the student is able to repeat the word, spell it, and then say it.	Repeat a word read by the teacher, spell it, and then say the word	Lesson 91

STORIES: DECODING — ORAL STORY READING   Range of Lessons: 1-160

Purpose of the track	Behavioral objectives	The student is asked to	First appears in
To teach the student to read a story accurately at a normal rate	When given a story, the student is able to read it aloud the fast way.	Read aloud as a group the title and first three sentences of a story and then, taking turns, read aloud individually one or more of the remaining sentences in the story	Lesson 1
		Taking turns, read aloud individually from the title to the end of a story	Lesson 81
		Taking turns, read aloud individually from the title to the circled 5 with no more than five errors for the group, and then read aloud individually the rest of the story	Lesson 84

Purpose of the track	Behavioral objectives	The student is asked to			First appears in
To teach the student to read with increased speed and accuracy	The student reads a previously read selection in a specified period of time with an error limit.	Read out loud at the following rates without exceeding the error limits:			
		Words per minute	Number of minutes	Error Limit	
		43	2.5	3	Lesson 5
		42	2.5	3	Lesson 10
		39	2.5	3	Lesson 15
		41	2.0	3	Lesson 20
		43	3.0	4	Lesson 25
		52	2.0	3	Lesson 30
		50	2.5	4	Lesson 35
		47	2.0	3	Lesson 40
		52	2.5	4	Lesson 45
		52	2.0	3	Lesson 50
		52	2.0	3	Lesson 55
		52	2.5	4	Lesson 60
		54	2.5	4	Lesson 65
		55	2.0	3	Lesson 70
		58	2.0	4	Lesson 75
		60	2.0	4	Lesson 80
		60	2.0	5	Lesson 85
		60	2.0	5	Lesson 90
		60	2.0	5	Lesson 95
		60	2.0	5	Lesson 100
		60	2.0	5	Lesson 105
		(continued)			

Purpose of the track	Behavioral objectives	The student is asked to	First appears in
		Read out loud at the following rates without exceeding the error limits:	

Words per minute	Number of minutes	Error Limit	
70	2.0	5	Lesson 110
70	2.0	5	Lesson 115
75	2.0	5	Lesson 120
75	2.0	5	Lesson 125
75	2.0	5	Lesson 130
80	2.0	5	Lesson 135
80	2.0	5	Lesson 140
80	2.0	5	Lesson 145
90	2.0	5	Lesson 150
90	2.0	5	Lesson 155
90	2.0	5	Lesson 160

STORIES: STORY COMPREHENSION — ORAL   Range of Lessons: 1-160

Purpose of the track	Behavioral objectives	The student is asked to	Range of lessons
To teach the student to focus on the meaning of a story while reading	When reading or re-reading a story, the student is able to answer comprehension questions interjected by the teacher.	Answer factual questions about the story	Lesson 1
		Answer a question by repeating a sentence or quotation	Lesson 1
		Answer a question by expressing an opinion or summarizing events	Lesson 1

STORIES: STORY COMPREHENSION — WRITTEN   Range of Lessons: 1-160

Purpose of the track	Behavioral objectives	The student is asked to	First appears in
To teach the student to focus on the meaning of a story through written exercises	When given a question or an incomplete item on a story previously read, the student is able to complete the exercise by remembering the story.	Circle the word or words in response to a written question	Take-Home 1
		Write in a blank the word or words in response to a written question	Take-Home 48
		Follow written instructions to answer a question or to complete an item	Take-Home 121
To teach the student to retain information	When given a written question or an incomplete item on a story that has been read in an earlier lesson, the student is able to complete the exercises by remembering the story.	Write in a blank the word or words in response to a written question	Take-Home 101

STORIES: PICTURE COMPREHENSION   Range of Lessons: 1-160

Purpose of the track	Behavioral objectives	The student is asked to	First appears in
To teach the student the relationship between a story and a picture	When the group has read a story, the student is able to predict what will be seen in a related picture and answer questions about the contents of the picture.	Answer an oral question, predicting what will be in a picture	Lesson 1
		Answer oral questions based on the content of the story and the details in the picture	Lesson 1

STORIES: RULE REVIEW   **Range of Lessons: 147-160**

Purpose of the track	Behavioral objectives	The student is asked to	First appears in
To teach the student to apply information from story to story	When asked about a rule from an earlier story, the student is able to repeat that rule.	Say a rule from an earlier story	Lesson 147

STORIES: READ THE ITEMS   **Range of Lessons: 3-94**

Purpose of the track	Behavioral objectives	The student is asked to	First appears in
To teach the student to read and follow written instructions	When given written instructions, the student is able to read the instructions and respond appropriately.	Read instructions and respond in a specified way to the teacher's designated actions or words	Lesson 3

Purpose of the track	Behavioral objectives	The student is asked to	First appears in
To teach the student how to write the symbols that represent sounds	When given a printed symbol previously introduced, the student is able to write the symbol	Write the following symbols:	
		wh	Take-Home 1
		m	Take-Home 1
		th	Take-Home 1
		r	Take-Home 1
		sh	Take-Home 1
		a	Take-Home 1
		n	Take-Home 2
		o	Take-Home 2
		i	Take-Home 3
		w	Take-Home 3
		s	Take-Home 3
		t	Take-Home 3
		v	Take-Home 3
		y	Take-Home 4
		u	Take-Home 4
		e	Take-Home 4
		ē	Take-Home 5
		b	Take-Home 8
		c	Take-Home 8
		d	Take-Home 8
		(continued)	

Purpose of the track	Behavioral objectives	The student is asked to	First appears in
		Write the following symbols:	
		f	Take-Home 8
		g	Take-Home 9
		h	Take-Home 9
		J	Take-Home 9
		k	Take-Home 13
		l	Take-Home 13
		ā	Take-Home 16
		ō	Take-Home 16
		ū	Take-Home 19
		z	Take-Home 19
		p	Take-Home 20
To teach the student to print words and sentences	When given a sentence, the student is able to print the sentence.	Trace a dotted version of a sentence and then print it freehand	Take-Home 3

TAKE-HOME EXERCISES: PICTURE COMPREHENSION

Range of Lessons: 1-25

Purpose of the track	Behavioral objectives	The student is asked to	First appears in
To teach the student the relationship between a story and a picture	When given incomplete items that go with a picture, the student is able to read and complete the items by looking at the picture.	Write the word to complete an item, using an initial consonant as a prompt	Take-Home 1

TAKE-HOME EXERCISES:
READING COMPREHENSION PASSAGES   **Range of Lessons: 8-160**

Purpose of the track	Behavioral objectives	The student is asked to	First appears in
To give the student practice in silent reading comprehension	When given a reading passage of a story or factual information, the student is able to read the passage silently and do written exercises relating to it.	Read a passage and related exercises aloud in a group and circle the answers to the exercises	Take-Home 8
		Read a passage and related exercises silently and circle the answers to the exercises	Take-Home 14
		Read a passage and related exercises aloud in a group and write the answers to the exercises	Take-Home 41
		Read a passage and related exercises silently and write the answers to the exercises	Take-Home 48
		Read a story passage and related exercises silently and follow written instructions to complete the exercises	Take-Home 121
		Read a factual passage and related exercises silently and follow instructions to complete the exercises	Take-Home 132

TAKE-HOME EXERCISES: FOLLOWING INSTRUCTIONS   **Range of Lessons: 18-120**

Purpose of the track	Behavioral objectives	The student is asked to	First appears in
To teach the student to follow written instructions	When given a circle or a box or both, the student is able to mark in, under, over, or next to the figure according to written instructions.	Mark in the specified places with letters, numbers, figures, or words	Take-Home 18
	When given a sentence in a box, the student is able to mark the sentence according to written instructions.	Mark the sentence in the specified places according to written instructions	Take-Home 47

TAKE-HOME EXERCISES: STORY PICTURE ITEMS   **Range of Lessons: 61-94**

Purpose of the track	Behavioral objectives	The student is asked to	First appears in
To teach the student the relationship between a story and a picture	When given a story-picture in the storybook, the student is able to read and answer questions about the picture.	Write answers to written questions by referring to details of the picture	Take-Home 61

TAKE-HOME EXERCISES: PICTURES DEDUCTIONS   **Range of Lessons: 95-147**

Purpose of the track	Behavioral objectives	The student is asked to	First appears in
To teach the student deductive thinking	When given a written rule, the student is able to read it and select pictures to which the rule applies.	Apply a simple rule Apply a rule with two criteria	Take-Home 95 Take-Home 132

TAKE-HOME EXERCISES: WRITTEN DEDUCTIONS   **Range of Lessons: 123-160**

Purpose of the track	Behavioral objectives	The student is asked to	First appears in
To teach the student deductive thinking through reading comprehension	When given a written rule, the student is able to read it and apply it.	Answer the question by applying the rule to a sentence Answer the question by applying the rule to a series of sentences	Take-Home 123 Take-Home 148

Spelling Note: There are 79 lessons in the *Reading Mastery II* spelling program. In these 79 lessons, and in the first 79 lessons of the reading program, the children spell by sounds rather than by letter names. At lesson 83 in the reading program, the children are introduced to all the letter names and begin the transition from spelling by sounds to spelling by letter names. By lesson 85, they are ready to begin a spelling program that is independent of the reading program.

SPELLING: SOUND WRITING   **Range of Lessons: 1-79**

Purpose of the track	Behavioral objectives	The student is asked to	First appears in
To give the student practice in writing sounds	When the teacher says one or more sounds, the student is able to repeat and write the sound or sounds.	Write the following sounds:	Spelling Lesson
		h	1
		s	1
		r	1
		a	1
		e	1
		t	1
		m	3
		n	4
		f	5
		i	8
		d	15
		p	16
		g	17
		b	18
		o	22
		c	22
		w	27
		l	28
		u	30
		(continued)	

Purpose of the track	Behavioral objectives	The student is asked to	First appears in
	When the teacher writes a sound combination on the board, the student is able to say the sound and write the letters that represent the sound.	Write the following sound combinations:	Spelling Lesson
		th	11
		ar	17
		sh	23
		ing	31
		al	50
		wh	59
		er	66
		ck	77
	When the teacher says a sound combination, the student is able to say the sound and write the letters that represent the sound.	Write the following sound combinations:	Spelling Lesson
		th	14
		ar	19
		sh	26
		ing	33
		al	53
		wh	62
		er	69
		ck	79

Purpose of the track	Behavioral objectives	The student is asked to	First appears in
To give the student practice in hearing and writing the sounds in words	When a word is presented, the student is able to write the sounds in the word.	Read a word, say the sounds in the word, and write the word	Lesson 1
		Say the sounds in a word the teacher has said and write the word	Lesson 4
		Say the sounds in an irregular or difficult word after the teacher has said the sounds and write the word	Lesson 4
		Read a sound combination word, say the sounds in the word, and write the word	Lesson 12
		Think about the sounds in a word the teacher has said and write the word	Lesson 15

SPELLING: SENTENCE WRITING
Range of Lessons: 21-79

Purpose of the track	Behavioral objectives	The student is asked to	First appears in
To give the student practice in spelling and writing words in sentences.	When the teacher dictates a sentence, the student is able to repeat the sentence slowly and then write the sentence with punctuation at the end.	Say and write one sentence	Lesson 21
		Say and write two sentences	Lesson 36
		Say and write three sentences	Lesson 72

NOTES: